The riddle of Zorfendorf
    Castle
Author: Abbott, Tony.
Reading Level: 4 ^ MG

JIZ 87185

D1488117

THE SECRETS OF DROON

The Riddle of
Zorfendorf Castle

by Tony Abbott

Illustrated by David Merrell

Cover illustration by Tim Jessell

SCHOLASTIC INC.
New York Toronto London Auckland Sydney
Mexico City New Delhi Hong Kong Buenos Aires

For Dolores,
ever and always

For more information about the continuing saga of Droon,
please visit Tony Abbott's website at
www.tonyabbottbooks.com

ISBN-13: 978-0-439-67173-6
ISBN-10: 0-439-67173-6

15 14 13 12 11 10 9 8 7 6 5   10 11 12/0

Printed in the U.S.A.
First printing, April 2005

Contents

One

At the Beach

It was noon on a warm Saturday when Eric Hinkle sat down on a sunny beach with his friends Neal and Julie.

He looked around and smiled. "Guys, this is the life."

"I know," agreed Neal. "This beach has all my favorite stuff. Sun and fun and . . . what's the third thing? Oh, yeah. Cheeseburgers, hot dogs, onion rings, curly fries, potato chips, and vanilla shakes —"

Eric laughed. "That's like . . . six things!"

"Not the way Neal eats," said Julie. "He's the original human blender!"

Neal looked thoughtful for a moment. "Blender Boy. I like it!"

The beach near Eric's house was a narrow strip of sand at the edge of a small pond. On one side was a tiny concession stand. On the other was a parking lot. In between were kids and parents from his neighborhood, sunning and playing and having fun.

"The water is so beautiful," said Julie, gazing out at the far side of the pond, where their gym teacher, Mr. Frando, was tossing a large net into the water. "It's kind of like the color of sapphires."

"It's kind of like the Sea of Droon," Neal whispered. "Only in our world."

Eric smiled again. Droon was the mysterious and magical world he and his friends had discovered under his house one day. Droon was where they had met Princess Keeah, a powerful young wizard. It was where they helped her battle an evil sorcerer known as Lord Sparr.

And it was where Eric and Julie had gotten magical powers. Julie had gained the ability to fly and sometimes to change shape. Once, she had pretended to be the spider troll Max. Another time, she changed into Neal's mother, the town librarian. Eric himself was fast becoming an actual wizard with a full range of awesome powers.

Each time the friends descended the rainbow-colored staircase in his basement — and they had gone down those steps many times — things in Droon had gotten more fabulous, more exciting, and more dangerous.

Julie sighed. "Keeah would love this. Too bad she doesn't have much time to just hang out. Especially now that things are a little weird —"

"A lot weird," said Neal. He looked at the concession stand and frowned.

Eric felt the same way.

Things in Droon really had gotten strange.

First of all, Sparr had recently woken a four-armed, three-eyed, bull-headed beast named Ko from a four-century nap. Now, Ko ruled over an empire of fearsome beasts.

Stranger still, in waking Ko up, Sparr himself had been transformed into a boy. He was now on their side, helping them stop Ko from turning Droon into his smelly Dark Lands.

But there was more.

The great wizard Galen, who had helped Keeah and her friends keep Droon free since the very beginning, was now gone. He had disappeared months before in a city called Ut.

"I can't wait for Galen to come back," said Eric. "We sure need him now."

"The Ring of Midnight will help us find him," said Julie.

Right. The amazing Ring of Midnight.

That was another weird thing.

The kids had recently discovered a large silver ring. They had no idea what the Ring was for, but when an image of Galen himself had appeared in the middle of it, everyone realized that the Ring might be the key to finding him.

Eric expected to be called back to Droon at any minute to start the search. "I packed the magic soccer ball in case Keeah sends for us."

"At least some things haven't changed," said Julie. "The ball still calls us to Droon.

And the staircase still takes us. I can't wait to go —"

"Maybe I'll get in line now," said Neal.

"Get in line? For the staircase?" asked Eric.

Neal shook his head. "For lunch. The concession stand is getting really busy."

He bounced up from the blanket, then pointed across the pond. "But call me if Mr. Frando catches any fish sticks out there!"

Eric and Julie sat watching as Neal worked his way inch by inch to the head of the food line. He was nearly at the counter when Eric turned his head and caught sight of a tall girl standing on the beach behind them. She had long, wavy hair and the darkest eyes he had ever seen.

Julie saw her, too. She made a low growling noise. "Meredith! She's everywhere."

Eric had to admit it. The girl *was* everywhere. She had just moved into a house on his street. She went to their school. She had even come to his house once. Meredith had only been around for a few days, and already Eric was certain she had heard them talking about Droon.

"Whenever I even *think* about Droon, she's there," said Julie. "We have to be careful."

Eric kept his eyes fixed on the girl. "Right," he whispered. "Careful. Because Droon has to stay a secret —"

Suddenly, Julie grabbed his arm. "Oh, my gosh, Eric, look —"

Eric turned to see Neal, his arms filled with trays and boxes and giant cups, heading straight for a hole some little kids had dug in the sand.

Eric nearly choked. "Oh, no! Neal!"

Neal peered over his food. "Coming!"

"He'll fall in!" said Julie.

Without thinking, Eric flicked the index finger of his right hand.

Zzzzzt! A single silver spark flew across the sand, whizzing past coolers and around beach chairs. Just as Neal lowered his foot — *pooomf!* — a small explosion of sand filled the hole.

Neal stepped on it firmly and kept walking.

Eric grinned. "Ha! That was awesome!"

"Not so awesome!" said Julie. "That nosy girl saw you! Meredith saw you! She's coming over here! And — look — the soccer ball!"

The magical soccer ball had begun to float up and away from the kids' blanket.

"Oh, no!" cried Eric. He tossed a beach towel over the ball and wrestled it to the ground.

Neal plopped down next to him, slurp-

ing a large milk shake. "Hey, what's going on?"

"Everything!" said Julie. "The new girl saw us! We're in really deep trouble now!"

But just when they expected her to stop at their blanket, Meredith ran past them and dived into the water. "That man needs help!" she yelled.

Everyone looked to the far side of the pond, where Mr. Frando was up to his neck, splashing around. "D-d-d-deep!" he cried.

The beach lifeguard jumped down from his chair and was in the water in a flash.

But before he was even halfway to Mr. Frando, Meredith was at the gym teacher's side, pulling him through the water toward the far shore.

Eric blinked. "She may be nosy, but she's an amazing swimmer. Mr. Frando is sure lucky."

"We're lucky, too, this time," said Julie.

She had begun throwing their beach stuff into her bag. "Maybe Meredith didn't see your spark, and maybe she didn't see the ball. But Keeah needs us. Neal, bring your food. We're going. Now!"

Without another word, the three friends took off from the beach, racing through backyards and darting down driveways until they bounded up the back steps of Eric's house.

Out of breath, Eric entered his kitchen and paused to listen. "The coast is clear. Let's go!"

They hustled down the basement stairs. Eric set the magic soccer ball on his father's workbench and turned to his friends. "Sorry, guys. Using powers at the beach was dumb. I know I need to be more careful."

"We all have to be careful," said Julie as they piled into a small closet under the stairs. She closed the door behind them.

"We can't let anyone know about Droon. Ever."

"True," said Neal. "But I'm glad you saved my lunch, Eric." He popped the last onion ring in his mouth, dusted his hands, and flicked off the ceiling light.

Whoosh! A bright light blazed, and the closet floor became the top step of a staircase glittering with every color of the rainbow.

"So awesome!" Eric whispered.

The three friends descended the stairs. Before long, they were surrounded by a thick fog. When the staircase ended, they found themselves in total darkness. They stepped onto a floor.

"We're in a room of some kind," said Julie.

Neal pinched his nose. "A smelly room. We aren't in a supply closet, are we?"

When their eyes had adjusted to the

dark, the three kids spied a faint outline ahead of them.

"We'll know soon enough," said Eric. "There's a door." He groped around carefully until he found a handle, then turned it slowly. The door opened on a corridor that was all black except for bright green flames leaping up from a cauldron at the ceiling.

"Green fire," whispered Neal. "Don't beasts like green — oh!"

Just then, a giant gray snail with dark red eyes slithered around the corner, heading straight toward them.

For the third time that morning, Eric nearly choked.

"Oh, no!"

Two

Playing with Models

Just as the giant snail raised its beady red eyes — *fwoop!* — the kids were yanked back into the room they had just left.

"Whoa —" gasped Eric.

"Hush!" said a quiet voice. "It's only us!"

Flish! A violet spark sizzled in the darkness. In its glow, the three friends saw the smiling face of a girl with long blond hair.

"Keeah!" whispered Julie.

"And not a moment too soon!" said the princess. "I think we almost lost you!"

"We?" said Neal.

"Ahem! Khan at your service!" squeaked a purple, pillow-shaped creature by Keeah's side. Khan was king of the Lumpies of Lumpland.

"Me, too, of course!" chirped a third voice. The smiling, pug-nosed face of Max, the spider troll, leaned into the spark's tiny light. He wore a small cape of bright green cloth.

"So, you got my message on your soccer ball," said Keeah as she pressed her ear against the door.

"Everyone else almost did, too," said Eric. "Because of me —"

"Because of saving my lunch," said Neal.

"Because sometimes," said Julie, "Eric's not very careful!"

"We *all* have to be careful now," said Khan, sniffing the door. "We are in the palace of Emperor Ko himself!"

Neal gulped loudly. "Ko's home? Where he lives? Oh, man. I think I just swallowed my brain!"

Julie chuckled. "Neal, I always knew your brain was in your stomach!"

Peeking out the door next to Keeah, Eric saw the giant snail glide down the corridor and pass out of view.

Ko's beasts were fiercer than anything they had battled in Droon before. They seemed to have very dull brains, but they were large and nasty. Their skin and fur and scales were mostly the color of ash. Eric had noticed that they smelled like something stored in a wet basement.

But perhaps most frightening was that each beast had fiery red eyes.

"Shouldn't we be getting out of here?" asked Neal. "I mean, like, now?"

Max chuckled softly. "Interesting thing about Ko's palace. It happens to fly five hundred feet in the air. Keeah —"

The princess went to the far side of the room and flicked her fingers at the wall.

Pop! A tiny porthole opened, and a blast of warm air rushed in from a desert far below.

Neal nodded. "Okay. Fine. Never mind!"

"Besides," said Khan, peering into the corridor, "we must find out what Ko is planning. The coast is stinky but clear. Let's move!"

Since Lumpies have a strong sense of smell, Khan led the others into the corridor. He sniffed, nodded, and pointed left. "This way!"

Eric, Julie, Neal, Keeah, and Max started down the hallway after Khan.

"How did you get inside this place any-way?" Julie asked.

"Last night, I spotted something streak-ing across the night sky," the Lumpy king whispered. "It landed in my desert."

Neal glanced at Eric. "Like a flying saucer!"

The little group turned another corner.

"Of course, Khan came to Jaffa City right away to tell me," said Keeah.

"Indeed," said Khan excitedly. "And we all came back here. Sparr came, too. No sooner had we all snuck aboard, when — *zoom-zoom!* — this butter dish took off again!"

"Flying saucer," Neal corrected him.

"Exactly!" said Khan. "Sparr knew in-stantly it was none other than Ko's flying palace!"

"So Sparr is here somewhere?" said Julie.

Max nodded as they followed Khan

around the next corner. "As soon as we crept on board, Sparr said he began to remember things. Things about Ko. He left us right away to investigate!"

"I hope he hasn't gotten himself into trouble," said Keeah.

Eric shot a look at the princess. "No kidding. I keep hoping that being a kid again and being with us will keep him *out* of trouble."

They all hoped that Sparr would not grow up to become the sorcerer they had once known. But they had to admit that the boy was mysterious. He had knowledge of things they knew little about.

Over the weeks they had been together, Eric had felt that there were two different sides of Sparr. One good. One bad. And the two Sparrs were battling each other to see who would win.

Keeah stopped outside a large hatchway.

"I don't have to be a Lumpy to smell the beasts in here. Their scent is too strong."

"Beasts aren't big into showering, are they?" said Neal.

"Not so much," said Keeah. She leaned on the hatch, opening it a crack, and they all peeked in.

Inside was a giant, round room. The ceiling was high and black. Dark-colored tapestries were draped on the walls, and black cauldrons hung from the ceiling. All but the center cauldron were blazing with the same deep green flames.

The giant snail they had seen earlier was standing erect now, looking down on something in the center of the room. Next to it stood a gray-furred beast that looked like a lion with spikes running down its back. Other beasts were crowded together, too. They were all facing away from the door and following the snail's gaze.

"What's so interesting?" whispered Julie. "A foosball game we can't see?"

"I see *that* plain enough!" snarled Max.

He was pointing at the terrible symbol of Ko. It was an upside-down triangle with two horns curving up from it. Three smaller triangles set inside the larger one were like the three eyes in Emperor Ko's head.

The symbol was on everything. It was woven into the tapestries, emblazoned on the flaming cauldrons, tiled on the floor, and painted on the ceiling.

"Ko sure likes to label his stuff," said Julie. "It's like *don't touch — or else*."

"Well," said Khan with a low chuckle, "I'm going to touch! If most of the beasts are in this room, no one will stop a little purple pillow from messing with Ko's flying soup bowl —"

"Saucer," whispered Eric.

"Exactly!" said Khan. "Every ship runs

on something. I'll find out what Ko's ship runs on — and I'll wreck it! Neal, come with me. We have a little bit of *touching* to do!"

Neal grinned. "Anything to leave this beastie playroom. Don't save me a seat —"

"We won't," said Julie. "Good luck!"

Neal and the Lumpy king trotted to the corner, edged around it, and disappeared.

While the beasts' backs were still turned, Keeah slipped into the room and hid behind one of the tapestries. She held it open for the others, and one by one they followed her.

Once they were safely hidden, they popped their heads out again. And they finally saw what all the beasts were staring at. In the middle of the room, on a large table, sat a miniature model of Droon, with tiny castles, cities, rivers, deserts, and mountains.

Even from his hiding place, Eric knew the model was magical, for everything on it moved. Tiny birds flew over Jaffa City. Golden monkeys swung through the trees of the Bangledorn Forest. Wind rippled the Sea of Droon, whipping up little white waves.

"Oh . . ." Keeah groaned. She pointed to a thick mass of smoky air that was building up at the border of the Dark Lands. It was edging slowly toward the free part of Droon.

As Eric watched, he felt his wizard power moving into his fingertips.

"Keeah, it won't happen. We won't let it," he whispered.

The beasts' mumbling quieted as a four-winged dragon entered from a far door.

"Gethwing!" grunted the beasts.

It was the terrible moon dragon the kids had seen twice before. His black scales glistened in the light from the green flames, and his red eyes glowed fiercely.

He hissed a sharp command, and the beasts bowed instantly to the floor.

"Oh, dear," whispered Max, shuddering.

Gethwing turned to look over his shoulder.

Eric felt his knees weaken. A chill ran down his neck. The room went suddenly cold.

Ko, Emperor of the Dark Lands, ruler of the beasts of Goll, swept into the room.

Ko was eight feet tall, with massive shoulders, four arms, and a great big bull's head. Between his two fiery horns sat a golden crown in the shape of a snake.

Ko spoke. "*Meth-ka-tahna-ro-Sparr?*"

His voice sounded like muffled thunder.

"Sparr?" whispered Julie. "Did he say *Sparr*?"

"Emperor," Gethwing replied in a low,

hissing snarl, "the time for the boy has not yet come. It will be soon. Not much longer . . ."

"Soon?" Eric muttered. "Soon for *what*?"

Nodding once, Ko moved to the table.

The other beasts, as fearsome as they were, seemed afraid of Ko. Still bowing, they quickly shifted away to give him room.

Ko loomed over the model of Droon, his three eyes resting on a single white castle nestled in a region of flat meadows.

"Then . . . the key is there!" Ko breathed with a deep rumble. "Zorfendorf!"

Keeah's face went pale. "Zorfendorf?" she whispered. "That's one of Droon's royal castles. It has a long and glorious history. What does Ko want there?"

"I'm sure he's not interested in checking out a book from its famous collection!" Max snarled.

Eric remembered their one brief visit to

Zorfendorf Castle. Its massive library of thousands of books was the finest in all of Droon.

Zorfendorf? But why? What's there for Ko?

As the beasts bent over the tiny castle, Eric felt Julie tense up beside him.

"Look . . ." she said softly, staring wide-eyed at something moving above Ko's head.

The largest of the ceiling cauldrons — the unlit one — was beginning to swing back and forth. And when it swung, it squeaked.

Errch . . . errch . . .

"Someone's hiding up there!" said Julie.

"Not for long," said Eric. "That cauldron's going to . . . to . . ."

All of a sudden — *whooom!* — the cauldron dropped from the ceiling, slammed onto the model, and rolled onto the floor with a tremendous crash.

The beasts leaped back as a boy with fins behind his ears tumbled out and bounced up among them. "Uh, sorry. Did I do that?"

"SPARRRR!" Ko roared. Black flames spurted out of his horns.

Gethwing stretched himself to his full, terrifying height. Then he leaped for the boy.

"Sparr — watch out!" cried Keeah. She jumped out from behind the tapestry and aimed her fingers at the moon dragon.

Kla-bamm! A violet beam struck Gethwing's chest, pushing him back against Ko.

"Sorry to blast and run," said Eric, "but —" *Blam! Blam!* He sprayed sparks at the other beasts. Then he rushed to Sparr, grabbed him, and pulled him to the door.

"That's our cue to run!" shouted Julie. She and Max dashed out the door.

Keeah followed them, then turned one

last time and sent blasts across the ceiling. *Whoom! Whoom!* The cauldrons fell and spilled flame everywhere.

"Thanks for the save!" said Sparr as the kids charged down the corridor.

"We're not saved yet!" said Keeah. "Khan! Khan —"

But the little Lumpy king was already there, racing around the corner with Neal.

"We found the engine room!" squeaked Khan. "This palace runs on lightning, you know —"

"Not for long!" said Neal. "I don't think the jam will hold forever —"

Sparr blinked. "Jam? What did you do?"

Neal shook his head. "Don't ask!"

Vrrrrr! The great flying palace tilted suddenly. It wobbled and dipped.

"Ha-ha!" laughed Khan. "It's working!"

But the hallway soon filled with beasts,

drooling and growling. Ko was at their head, his three eyes blazing with rage.

"Sorry," said Keeah, "but we can't stay!"

Sparr pointed to where the floor and the wall met. "Eric, Keeah, blast right there!"

Together, the three of them blasted a small hole through to the outside. *Kla-blammm!*

Warm air rushed into the corridor.

"They say Lumpland has the softest sand of all!" cried Khan as the palace lurched again. It was plummeting toward the desert below.

"I guess we'll find out soon enough!" shouted Keeah. "Jump!"

As the beasts charged, the kids squeezed through the opening and leaped from the flying palace, yelling at the top of their lungs.

"Ahhhhhhh —"

Three

The Big Red Book

Luckily, the kids didn't have far to fall.

Ko's palace was just a few feet above the ground at the moment they'd jumped. Eric, Keeah, Julie, Neal, Max, Khan, and Sparr plopped onto the soft desert dunes and rolled to a stop.

As the palace jerked wildly up again, Eric saw it from the outside for the first time. It was large and black and ugly, a flying city with high walls and tall towers coiling up from its shiny surface.

Khan bounced to his feet. "The beasts will squeal when they see we've used all their spoons!"

Julie sat up. "Beasts use *spoons*?"

"Not anymore!" said Neal with a chuckle.

Dusting herself off, Keeah hurried to the top of the nearest dune and whistled. A moment later, a group of six-legged, shaggy-haired creatures trotted up to them.

"Pilkas!" exclaimed Eric. "Our rides to Zorfendorf."

Keeah jumped onto the back of one pilka. "They brought us from Jaffa City this morning. When I left, my parents were trying to find out clues about the Ring of Midnight."

"Perhaps we shall meet up with them

soon," said Khan, climbing up next to Max on the smallest pilka. "For now, I suggest we ride like the wind to Zorfendorf. Hi-ya, ho!"

With Keeah in the lead, the seven friends raced over the sandy wastes of Lumpland. Before long, the desert gave way to miles of wide and rolling meadows.

As they galloped through plains of high grass, Eric turned to Sparr. "Ko wants you for something," he said. "Do you know what it is?"

The boy quickly shook his head. "Whatever it is, Gethwing said the time hasn't come yet. I just hope . . . I mean . . . I don't want to go back to Ko. Ever."

Eric shared a look with Keeah.

"Don't worry," she said. "You won't. We'll make sure of that."

They soon spotted the tip of a large tower peeping over the crest of a valley. As each mile passed, more of the giant white castle came into view. It stood in the center of a wide green plain. Its highest tower was surrounded by smaller towers and circled by thick walls of white stone.

"It's so beautiful!" said Julie.

"And centuries old, too," said Max. "So much history has happened here."

"Maybe that's why Ko wants to get in so badly," said Neal. "Maybe he left something here ages ago. Something mysterious."

Eric nodded. Zorfendorf was certainly mysterious. With all the adventures he and his friends had had in Droon, they had never met the castle's current ruler. In fact, Prince Zorfendorf had not been seen by anyone for as long as they could remember.

"Some say the prince is an explorer!" said Khan as the pilkas descended into the valley. "Or that he is trapped somewhere."

"Others say he never existed!" said Max.

Eric turned to Sparr as they rode. "Did you ever meet him?"

The boy shook his head. "I don't think so. But then, I'm beginning to forget some things I did as a grown-up. Instead, I remember more of when I was little. Like Ko's flying palace. I must have played there as a boy. The moment I saw it, I knew exactly how to get to his war room."

Keeah looked at Eric again. "Well, no matter what Ko wants here, Zorfendorf has been safe for centuries. We have to keep it that way."

When the castle guards saw the little group approaching the high walls, they opened the gates wide and cheered.

Keeah raised her hand, and the cheering stopped. "Zorfendorf is in danger —"

"Beasts are coming!" chirped Max.

"Led by Emperor Ko himself!" added Khan.

At that, the doors of the inner castle swung open, and a giant nearly twenty feet tall strode out. "Did someone say *danger*?"

"Thog!" cried Julie, spurring her pilka over to the giant.

Thog's kindly features brightened when he saw the children. He had large eyes, three floppy ears, and a big bald head. A long fur wrap hung from his shoulders to his knees. Thog was the keeper of Zorfendorf's library.

"Emperor Ko is coming," Keeah told him. "He wants something in Zorfendorf. But we don't know what it might be. . . . Wait — Thog, what's wrong?"

The giant frowned, scratched his ears, then looked up at the tower. "There is something," he said. "Follow me. To the Great Tower!"

As the castle's guards began arming themselves with staffs and shields, preparing for Ko's arrival, Thog led the children into the tower. It was flooded with sunlight. A set of stone steps spiraled up the inside of the tower, from the ground all the way to the open top, where a patch of blue sky was visible.

"There's nothing here but steps," said Neal, looking up. "What is the tower for?"

"A riddle I have never been able to answer," said Thog. "But come. Look at this."

Up the tower stairs they went, around and around, until they came to a narrow platform that ran around the top. The warm wind of the day blew across the tower with a low whistling sound.

"The view is incredible!" said Max, his orange hair blown back. His small cape flapped in the breeze.

"Thog, why are we here?" asked Keeah.

"You said we are in danger. I discovered

this only last week," said Thog. "I think it was hidden here for a moment such as this."

He paced four steps from the stairway, bent to the platform, and pulled up a loose stone. Underneath sat a large red book. Embossed in gold letters on its cover were the words *The History of Zorfendorf Castle*.

"A thick book!" said Max, rubbing his paws together. "It's because the castle's history goes way back. It should tell us everything!"

"Everything about what Ko wants here," added Julie.

Thog removed the book and laid it heavily on the tower wall.

"Maybe it will refresh my memory even more," said Sparr eagerly. "Let's read it."

As the guards called out more commands below, and the preparations for battle continued, Keeah lifted the book's large cover and turned to the first page.

It was blank.

So were the second and third.

In fact, all the pages of the big red book were blank except for the last one. Scribbled there were only a few lines in pale blue ink.

Max gasped. "I know that ink! I know that handwriting! My master Galen wrote that!"

"What does it say?" asked Sparr, leaning in.

Keeah moved her fingers across the page and began to read.

"'It is the eighth orbit of the second moon —'"

The princess stopped. "That's . . . six . . . no, seven years ago. Seven years ago."

She went on. "'I write this quickly, before I, too, fall under the spell. . . .'"

"What spell?" asked Eric.

"Keeah, keep reading," urged Sparr.

"'Among the tall grasses and sweet sea breezes of this valley, I discovered the Fifth River —'"

"What's the Fifth River?" asked Khan.

Thog blinked. "There are no rivers here."

"'Knowing that none other must ever find the river, I conjured a great castle from nothing —'"

"*Conjured* a great castle?" said Sparr, looking around at the massive stone walls. "Does he mean Zorfendorf? Conjured *from* nothing?"

"'Then I cast a spell over all of Droon. From this day forward, everyone will think this castle has always been here. And so, the Fifth River will remain a secret. The riddle of Zorfendorf Castle will be kept secret forever. The riddle of . . . the riddle of . . . what riddle? Ah, the spell has taken me now. . . . I go from here . . . this strange old castle . . . so old . . . so very . . . old. . . .'"

The writing trailed off, and Keeah stopped. She gazed at the vast white castle below them. "Does this mean that Zorfendorf is only . . . seven years old? Galen *created* this castle? And he made everyone think Zorfendorf has always been here?"

"Is that even possible?" asked Julie.

Neal frowned. "One thing's possible. Galen conjured me a headache. I'm having it now."

Sparr stood suddenly and stared out beyond the castle wall. Just coming into view was the tiny black smudge of Ko's palace.

"I don't know what it means or what it is," said Sparr, trembling. "But if Galen conjured Zorfendorf to hide the Fifth River, then *that's* what Ko is after."

"But how does Ko know about it?" asked Eric. "Galen made everyone forget."

"Even me," said Thog, scratching his head.

Sparr touched his ear fins lightly. Then he snorted a tiny laugh. "Of course! Everyone *did* forget that Zorfendorf wasn't old. Everyone except a creature that was under an ancient spell. A beast that was deep asleep. A beast named Ko."

Eric bent to the book again and noticed a tiny sketch at the bottom of the page. It showed four wiggly lines coming together like an X with a tiny circle in the center.

Under it were the words: *The Fifth River.*

"I don't get it," Eric said softly. "If these lines are four rivers coming together, where's the fifth? Besides, Thog says there aren't any rivers here. It's all too weird —"

"Weird, perhaps, but look!" exclaimed Khan. He pointed to a faint shadow wandering across the meadows. It looked like a forgotten path no one traveled anymore. Khan traced it all the way to Zorfendorf, where it disappeared under the castle walls.

"Maybe a river once flowed there," said Thog.

"Or still flows underground," said Keeah.

"There's one, too!" shouted Neal. He was standing across the platform, squinting at the ground below.

"And another one," called Julie, pointing at a third shadow wandering across the earth.

"Here, too!" Khan called out.

There were four shadows in all. The kids searched for signs of a fifth, but found none.

"Four is better than nothing," chirped Max. "Four underground rivers —"

"All leading under the castle," said Thog, looking from the ground to Galen's sketch. "And I know where they meet. Quickly! Follow me!"

Four

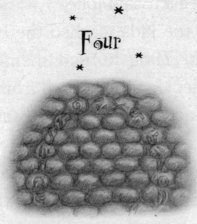

A Bunch of Riddles

The second-to-last thing the kids saw before Thog hurried them down the tower was the vast army of castle guards that had assembled along the wall.

The *very* last thing they saw was Ko's flying palace lurching and dipping in the sky, slowly approaching the castle.

"By my calculations," said Khan, "the tape will come undone in about an hour —"

"Tape?" said Thog.

"Don't ask!" said Julie.

When the kids reached the bottom of the tower, Thog hurried them into the main castle. He took a torch from the wall and descended a set of stairs that led under the floor.

As they wound their way through passages to the deepest levels of the castle, the group passed a dark room that was completely empty.

Thog stopped. "For as long as I can remember, this room has been called The Wizard's Sneeze."

Neal made a face. "What does that mean? That Galen came here when his nose was itchy?"

The Lumpy king peered in and chuckled. "Zorfendorf does have its riddles, doesn't it? Thog, if you please. Lead on!"

The giant continued down through the castle's dungeons. The halls became narrower and tighter. The stairs twisted and curved back on themselves, but always drove deeper into the earth.

"I still can't believe it," said Julie, running her hand along the ever-darkening walls. "The castle looks hundreds of years old!"

"Galen's charm is amazing," said Max. "Well, of course it is. He can do anything!"

The passages finally ended in a dark chamber that was completely closed at the end.

Thog stopped, his eyes full of fear. "Here."

The children looked at one another.

"This looks like a dead end," said Sparr.

"Not quite," said Keeah.

In the wavering shadows cast by Thog's torch, they could see marks carved into the wall in the shape of a high, arched doorway.

"Holy cow!" said Julie. "A magic door?"

The giant stepped back, a frown on his face.

"It's okay, Thog," said Eric. "We'll take it from here. The more we find out, the better we can all defend Zorfendorf against Ko."

The giant nodded firmly. "I'm needed to help defend against the attack. I'll come back when Ko is near." He left his torch with Keeah, then disappeared the way they'd come.

Julie stared at the marks on the wall. "I wish Galen had written more about the Fifth River before his spell made him forget."

"I think we'll find out soon," said Neal.

Holding the torch close with one hand, Keeah ran her fingers along the carvings.

The spider troll crouched next to her. "This is one of my master's spells. Princess, read it."

Eric listened closely as Keeah read the

words aloud. She started backward from the bottom right, up and around the top of the arch, and back down to the bottom left.

The words sounded like the calling of birds.

"Beautiful," said Khan.

"And powerful," added Max proudly. "My master Galen knows all kinds of spells."

Suddenly, the wall that looked hundreds of years old quivered, as if waves of heat rose from the floor in front of it. The dark stones went pale, almost white, then turned as clear as glass and vanished.

"Keeah, you did it," said Neal.

Even with Keeah's torch, the children could barely make out what lay beyond the opening. The sound of dripping water echoed inside.

Khan sniffed here and there. "Hmmm. It certainly smells old. And quite damp."

"Like a wet basement," said Julie, peering into the dark. "Kind of like the beasts' smell."

"Maybe," said Eric. He squinted ahead, trying to make out a shape in the gloom. His heart was thudding with excitement, as if something were about to happen.

And then it did.

At the exact moment that the children passed through the doorway — *whoooosh!* — a burst of cool, wet air blew Keeah's torch out.

They heard the low roar of water. As they entered the chamber, they felt it beneath their feet like the constant rumble of thunder.

Even in the darkness, the children could make out the shapes of four channels cut into the floor. One came from each corner of the room and met in the center to form a giant X.

Each channel was rushing with water.

"The four rivers we saw!" said Julie.

All of a sudden, a blinding silvery light burst in the dark room. The children froze.

"And the rivers meet *there*," said Sparr.

Eric staggered back. "There . . ."

The rivers met in the center of the room at the base of an enormous fountain. The fountain was made of brilliant white stones carved into fantastic shapes. It rose from the floor all the way to the ceiling.

"This is what Galen wished to hide forever?" said Max. "A big fountain?"

"A big, *dry* fountain?" said Neal.

For the fountain *was* dry. Even though the water rushed violently into its base, the fountain itself was covered with a thick layer of dust. Cobwebs were draped across it like ghostly curtains.

Eric estimated that the strange sculpture was at least fifteen feet high. On the

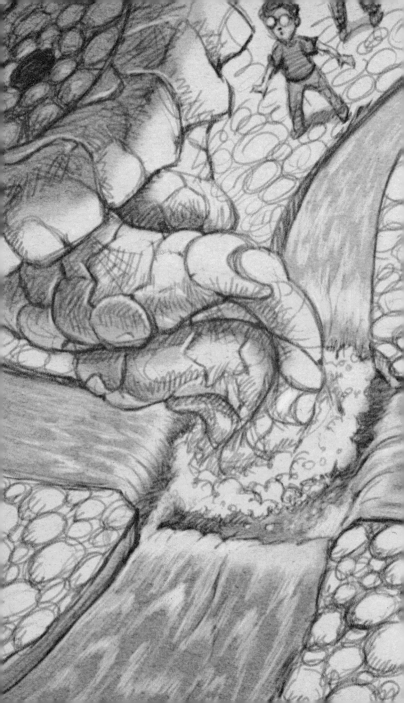

ceiling directly above it was a wide ring of white stars.

"Weirder and weirder," he muttered.

"A fountain right under the castle," said Khan, his hands on his hips. "Who would have believed it?"

Keeah turned to Sparr. "Do you know why Ko would want to find this?"

Sparr closed his eyes, then shook his head. He looked confused, troubled. "I almost remember. But no. I don't. . . ."

"Writing!" said Max excitedly. "There's writing on the fountain. But not Galen's writing. I've never seen this kind before!"

Everyone gathered around the row of carvings that twisted and coiled around the base of the fountain.

The more Eric stared at the figures, the more he imagined he could see the shapes of animals, trees, people, stars.

"Maybe it comes from the time when Ko

first ruled," said Khan, sniffing the strange writing. "Sparr, is it beast language?"

Eric turned. Sparr wasn't looking at the fountain. He was wobbling back and forth, his head hanging down, his eyes closed.

"Well, this is no language I've ever seen," said Keeah. "How are we going to read it? Maybe it's impossible —"

Sparr raised his head slowly, opening his eyes. "Not quite impossible," he said. "I can tell you what it says. . . ."

Five

The Magic Word

The fins behind Sparr's ears were getting redder by the moment. They almost glowed with their own deep fire. His eyes darkened and he seemed smaller than just minutes before, as if he were crouching under some heavy, invisible weight.

He knows the language! thought Eric.

Sparr looked at the others. "I guess no one else understands this. So I'll read it."

He knelt on the floor and, beginning

with a word that looked like four snakes arched and fighting, he slowly began to read.

"'Four rivers, one from each of the four seas of Droon, meet here and form a . . . fifth.'"

"The Fifth River!" said Max, looking around. "But where is it? It's not even here."

"There's more." Sparr moved to the far side of the fountain and kept reading. "'Its journey is for one alone. Speak only this last word, and the Fifth River will come. . . .'"

Eric stared at the symbols as Sparr spoke each one. Then he looked ahead to where a single character stood by itself.

It looked like a sun with wavy lines coming from it. Inside it were two crescent moons back to back. Crossing from left to right was a snake dotted from head to tail with stars.

Eric thought it looked like something he had seen somewhere a long time before.

Sparr frowned, closed his eyes, opened them again, and shook his head. "I don't know this word yet. Give me a minute —"

A distant shriek echoed in the chamber. Then a low gasp came from behind them.

Thog filled the doorway. His huge eyes widened when he saw the fountain. "The guards asked me to find you. Lizards. Lots of them. With wings of fire —"

"Wingsnakes!" said Sparr, rubbing his head suddenly. "I thought I smelled them on the ship. Ko always starts battles with them. We need to . . . need to . . ."

The sound of shrieking came again — louder this time. The wingsnakes were approaching.

"Oh, I'm coming! I know how to fight them!" Sparr joined Thog, then turned back to the others. "Guard this room until I come back. I don't know what the last word is, but I'm sure I can read it. Ko won't get his ugly claws on our fountain. This is amazing. Amazing!"

The shrieks grew louder, and Sparr rushed from the chamber with Thog. The children listened until the sound of their footsteps could no longer be heard.

"This is great," said Julie. "We find the big riddle of Zorfendorf, and it has to wait."

"At least Sparr knows this wacky language," said Neal. "We'd be sunk otherwise."

Eric followed the strange carvings from the beginning all the way to the large symbol at the end. He remembered the first few words his parents had ever taught him to read.

Staring at the sun, moons, stars, and that strange snake, his heart pounded in his chest.

If it did form a word, it was a word so different from every other he had ever learned.

"Wacky is right!," he murmured. "Too weird . . ."

And yet, as strange as the symbol was, some part of his brain tingled when he saw it.

Without thinking, his lips formed a word.

"*Ythra* —"

Everyone looked at him.

"Eric?" said Keeah, moving to him. "Did you just say something?"

He glanced at his friends, then back at the fountain. "Sorry," he said. "It's just . . . that word . . . I mean . . . it's . . ."

Tracing his fingers slowly over the carving, he said the word again.

"*Ythra.*"

Neal squinted at Eric. "Even supposing

you're right, do you have any idea what it means — whoa!"

They all noticed it at the same time. The circle of stars on the ceiling had begun to spin. As it did, the stones inside the circle spiraled away until the ceiling was completely open. The children looked up. They could see right up through the Great Tower to the blue sky above.

Keeah gasped. "Look at the fountain!"

At that moment, the rivers thundering beneath the floor suddenly burst up into the fountain, sloshing and crashing all the way up to the top.

"My goodness — look!" cried Khan.

A thin stream of water spurted noisily from the top, coiling like a thin rope up into the air.

But instead of falling back down again, the stream kept moving up. It flowed through the hole in the ceiling and straight up through the center of the tower, gaining power and speed as it went.

"The Fifth River!" Julie yelled over the roar of the water. "That's the Fifth River! Eric, you did it! *Ythra* is the magic word!"

With each passing second, the stream grew and thickened, first into a flow, then into a rush, streaming up the tower to the sky above.

Max staggered into Khan. "Oh, marvelous!"

"Eric!" said Keeah, transfixed by the rushing water. "It must mean something. Where does the river go? What does *Ythra* mean?"

Eric didn't know how he knew, but he *did* know. "The Upper World," he said.

Suddenly, the fountain began to change. All the stones moved at once — *foom-foom-foom!* — shifting up, dropping down, turning, refitting themselves into new positions. Finally, a long, sleek shape burst up from inside the fountain and bobbed on the surface of the river.

"What is that —" Eric started, but when the thing moved forward on the water, he knew what it was.

"A boat!" he said. "A boat made of stone!"

"This is unbelievable magic!" said Keeah, unable to take her eyes off it.

"Amazing!" gasped Julie. "Impossible!"

And yet there it was, right before their eyes: a long, hollow vessel, rounded in the back and tapered to a point on the front end.

It faced the sky above and bobbed up and down, as if begging them to climb aboard.

"This is what Ko is after," said Keeah. "The Fifth River goes to the Upper World! Ko wants to invade the Upper World!"

No sooner had she said that than a

flock of snakelike beasts soared over the tower above them. The snakes were long and thin, with ash-gray scales running from their flat heads to their spiked tails. Their wings were ragged and dark and tipped with bright red flames.

"Ko has begun his attack!" said Khan.

The shrieking snakes swarmed around the place where the river burst from the tower. *Eeeee! Eeeee!*

"We can't let Ko win!" said Keeah. "We have to . . . we have to . . . get in! Everyone! Climb the fountain. Get into the boat!"

"Sparr will be mad we left him!" said Neal.

"Ko can't have that boat!" said Eric. "All aboard, before it leaves. Hurry —"

He scrambled up the fountain, sloshing through the water and into the stone boat. Keeah staggered up behind him. Julie and

Neal helped each other up and together pulled Max and Khan after them.

As soon as they were in — *vooooom!* — the boat leaped up and away from the fountain.

Eeeeee! Eeeeee! The flying beasts shrieked and swarmed around the tower's top.

But the boat kept going. It gathered speed as it raced up the inside of the tower. It was heading right for the fiery wing-snakes.

"Maybe now's the time to tell you all," yelled Neal. "I'm not really a boat guy!"

"You are now!" shouted Julie. "Hold on!"

Six

Up, Up, and Away!

Up through the Great Tower they splashed, nearly sinking time and again into the rushing river, but popping up at the last second.

"Who's driving this thing?" cried Neal, holding tight.

"Not me!" said Julie.

"Not anyone!" shrieked Max. "The boat is driving itself!"

"Excuse me, but nobody likes a soggy pillow!" squealed Khan. "Getting wet here!"

When they shot up from the tower, they saw Sparr atop the castle wall below.

The boy jumped when he saw them. "Hey, wait! Wait for me!"

"We can't!" cried Eric. "We —"

Eeeee! The swarm of wingsnakes attacked.

"Oh, no, you don't!" shouted Sparr. He ran across the wall, firing sizzling blasts at the flying snakes, from one hand first, then the other, then both. *Blam! Blam! Blam!*

"Stay away from my friends!" he yelled.

And the flying snakes did, fleeing back to Ko's palace while the boat shot into the clouds, leaving Zorfendorf far behind.

"Ha!" Neal yelled. "Thanks to Sparr, those overheated earthworms will never find us!"

The fluffy pink clouds turned black as the children sped higher and higher.

"Even *we* won't find us," said Keeah.

Darkness surrounded them like a tunnel. The boat dipped and twisted, flying faster and faster over the rushing water. Waves surged over the bow and sprayed up over the sides.

"Ohhh!" groaned Khan. "I smell danger and it's coming from — everywhere!"

Suddenly, the dark water ahead of them began to turn light blue. Eric felt his heart thump suddenly. It was a color, he thought, that reminded him of . . . sapphires.

"Oh, no!" he said. "The pond! We're coming up in our pond! Mr. Frando will see us! The lifeguard will see us. *That girl will see us!*"

"We need a distraction!" said Neal.

"I have an idea," said Julie. "Eric, Keeah, blast now!"

Just as the boat broke the surface, the two wizards aimed blasts at the water.

At the same moment, Julie jumped up and out of the boat.

Only it was no longer Julie that anyone saw, but a dazzling orange fish, spinning up as if it had leaped right out of the water!

As Mr. Frando, Meredith, and the lifeguard gaped at the big fish, the kids, Max, and Khan jumped from the boat and scrambled to shore.

By the time Julie dived back into the pond, the rest of the kids were safely behind a cluster of pine trees. The stone boat sank under the surface of the pond and disappeared. A moment later, Julie was running toward them. She was soaking wet.

"Julie, thanks, that was amazing," said Keeah. "And beautiful, too!"

Julie blushed. "Hey, I try."

"I wish *I* could change into a fish," grumbled Khan. "It's less noticeable than a pillow-shaped king. We have visitors!" He pointed to the people coming toward them.

Eric glanced at his wet friends: a Droon princess in a turquoise-blue tunic, an eight-legged spider troll, and a purple pillow, wearing a big gold crown.

"I think we have a problem," he said.

Keeah chuckled. "I know what to do!" She whispered something quickly, and everyone jumped into position.

In a blur, Max found a long stick, poked it into the sand, climbed up, spread out his eight legs, and whipped his cape over him. Khan plopped facedown, hiding his arms and legs, while Keeah twirled.

When Mr. Frando, the lifeguard, and Meredith finally reached them, they found Eric and Julie relaxing under a big green umbrella. Neal was leaning back on a big pillow, while Keeah was covered with a bright blue beach blanket.

Julie smiled at Keeah. "So, cousin Kee-Kee, how do you like our pond?"

"Nice," said the princess. "Big waves, strange fish, but nice."

Mr. Frando squinted at the kids. "Strange fish, all right. I've never seen anything like *that* before!" Then he squeezed the water from his hat and tramped away with the lifeguard.

Meredith frowned. "If I didn't know better, I'd say you were all up to something."

"Up to something?" asked Eric as he put his hands behind his head. "Like what?"

The new girl looked from one to the other. "I don't know. You seem a little too goofy."

Neal grinned as he leaned back on Khan. "Hey, we try!"

"Uh-huh," she said. She stared at them for a long moment, then turned and walked back to the beach.

When Meredith was gone, Khan bounced up and brushed sand from his face. Max wiggled all over and set his cape into place. Keeah gave the blanket a twirl, and it vanished.

"Thanks," said Eric. "We could have been in deep trouble."

"We're already in deep trouble," said Keeah. "If the boat returned to Droon, Ko could get it. We need to get back now."

"The staircase," said Neal. "Let's go."

Eric looked at Keeah, Max, and Khan. "Okay. But let's go the back way."

The friends scurried deep into the woods and worked their way around the pond.

"Ko's not only after the boat," said Eric as they darted behind a garage. "He's after Sparr, too."

"And why does Ko want him back so bad?" asked Neal. "I mean, Sparr brought him back to life. Isn't that enough?"

Ever since he had heard Ko and Gethwing talking on the flying palace, Eric had been wondering the same thing.

"Maybe Ko's afraid of Sparr," said Julie. "Maybe he's afraid because with Sparr's help, we might actually beat Ko."

Eric's heart skipped a beat. If Sparr *could* help them defeat Ko, and he *could* grow up good, Droon might finally be at peace.

Keeah would be so happy! he thought.

But the princess was frowning.

"Or," she said, "what if Ko needs him for some big, dark magical thing? Maybe that's why Ko kidnapped him from the Upper World in the first place. You know, back when Sparr was a baby. And now that Ko's awake, he needs Sparr to help him put his evil plan into action."

Eric felt as cold as ice.

"I guess that's possible," he said. "Either way, we have to be sure Ko never gets him."

Looking both ways, they dashed across one last street and up to Eric's house.

Breathing hard, Eric pulled his back door open, listened, then nodded. "It's okay. No one's home. Come on."

Neal led the way down to the basement.

"How amazing!" whispered Khan as they crowded into the small room under the stairs. "Mrs. Khan and my little ones will not believe it! And you get to do this all the time!"

Smiling, Eric closed the door behind them. "It is pretty cool. Is everyone ready?"

"Ready!" said Keeah.

"Next stop, Zorfendorf!" said Julie. She reached up and turned off the light.

Whoosh! — the rainbow stairs appeared, right on cue. The six friends hurried down through a layer of wispy clouds. The stairs ended just above the plain in front of the castle.

"Ko's nearly here!" said Keeah. She pointed to the dark shape of the emperor's palace only a few hundred feet away. The wingsnakes Sparr had chased from the tower were massing for another attack.

"Oh, dear!" said Khan. "To the castle!"

But the moment they left the stairs, they heard pilkas whinnying behind them. Two riders were galloping toward them.

"I know those pilkas!" said Max, squinting.

"And I know those riders!" said Keeah. "My mother and father. Hurry! We've got to tell them everything!"

But the flock of wingsnakes was already overhead. They shrieked. They wailed.

Then they dived at the king and queen.

Seven

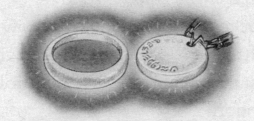

The Ring of Midnight

Eeeeee! Eeeeee! The flaming flying beasts swooped wildly at Keeah's parents.

"Eric, hurry!" shouted the princess.

She sent two quick blasts at the beasts. Eric followed with more. *Blam-blam! Blam-blam-blam-blam!* When Relna joined in, the sky blossomed with sparks.

The wingsnakes wailed and their red eyes burned, but they turned back to Ko's palace.

Keeah's parents rode swiftly to the kids.

"Mother, Father, are you all right?" asked Keeah, running breathlessly to them. "We've just been to the Upper World —"

Queen Relna nodded. "We know about the Fifth River! The Ring of Midnight told us. But it's not safe here. Quickly, to Zorfendorf!"

The small band hurried across the plains to the castle. "Open the gates!" yelled the guards when they saw them coming.

Sparr was waiting for the children inside. "Tell me everything!" he said. "Did the Fifth River really take you to the Upper World?"

"It did!" said Khan. "It was wondrous!"

"We almost got caught!" said Max.

"Sparr, children, everyone," said Relna, "into the castle. There is something we need."

"We'll explain as we go," said Zello. "Guards, be ready! There is no time to waste!"

The group entered the castle at a run. Relna led them down one set of stairs after another.

"Here is what we know," she said, sliding into a tight passage. "As we guessed, the Ring of Midnight is made of silver."

Zello pulled the large, bracelet-sized object from the pocket of his cape. "But it is unlike any silver known in the free part of Droon."

"Is it from the Dark Lands?" asked Keeah.

"It may be," said King Zello. "But that is not the amazing thing. While the Ring of Midnight has magical properties of its own, it is actually a part of another magical object."

The king and queen stopped above a set of stairs lit by the glow of a torch on the wall.

Zello held up the Ring, and Relna pulled a round white stone from inside her cloak.

"The Moon Medallion!" chirped Max.

Eric shivered. The Moon Medallion was a disk-shaped stone carved with strange symbols. He had seen it only once before, but he was aware of its awesome force.

Sparr stared at it. "Is that the magical medallion that belonged to Urik? It was his, wasn't it? It's beautiful."

"Yes," said Relna.

Eric knew that the Medallion's power was bound up with all three sons of Zara — Urik, Galen, and Sparr. He remembered too that it was Sparr himself who had fought Urik for the Medallion in the Upper World and had tried to use its power against Galen.

"The Ring of Midnight revealed little until we combined it with the Medallion," said Zello. "Now look at this!"

The king and queen joined the two objects, sliding the Medallion inside the Ring.

Click. The Ring fit around the Medallion as if it were a frame, holding it snugly. All of a sudden, the Medallion pulsed with a silvery light from within, and its shiny surface swam with tiny words.

"Wow!" said Neal. "It's like a whole book written in really small words —"

"A whole library!" said Zello. "There are millions of words here. From what we can tell so far, the Medallion, among other things, is a vast history of an old and forgotten magic!"

Gazing at the words flickering on the disk's surface, Eric realized that they were in the same language as those they had seen on the fountain.

"The Ring of Midnight is like a key," said the queen. She began to descend the stairs. "It unlocks some of the Medallion's many secrets and translates the words into a language we can understand."

Zello nodded. "There are, perhaps, other pieces yet to be found. So not all the Medallion's secrets can be revealed yet. It may take years to understand it all. But one story is clear. . . ."

The queen stopped at the bottom of the stairs to look at Sparr.

Trembling, he asked her, "What story?"

As the rumble of Ko's flying palace grew louder, Relna spoke. "We know that Galen created Zorfendorf to hide the fountain. But the fountain itself was created five centuries earlier in a moment of great need."

"Great need?" said Keeah. "What need?"

Now Relna and Zello were both looking at Sparr.

"The Medallion tells of a wizard long ago in Droon," said the king, picking up the story. "This wizard needed to send her innocent child to safety, to free him from a terrible beast —"

Sparr turned pale. "Her innocent child!"

"You, Sparr," said Zello. "You and your mother, Queen Zara, were kidnapped by Ko from the Upper World and brought to Droon because of your powers. Zara sought to send you away from him, to free you —"

Sparr nearly choked. "My mother was . . . here? She made the fountain . . . for me?"

The queen nodded sadly. "Zara was more powerful than we could ever believe. She charmed rivers from each corner of Droon to meet here. From them, she conjured the Fifth River and built a magical fountain."

"For me?" said Sparr again.

"For you," said Zello. "But she never got a chance to use it. She died in this very spot."

Sparr began to tremble. "Oh . . . oh . . ."

"Zara knew Ko was coming. So she made the fountain invisible with her final breath," continued the queen. "She must have hoped you could use it someday. After five hundred years, her invisibility spell faded. That was when Galen found the fountain."

"So he built the castle to hide it," said Julie softly. "This is too *amazing*!"

Looking at Sparr, Eric felt chills. The boy sorcerer wobbled as if ready to collapse.

"This attack is all my fault!" Sparr said finally. "My mother created the river to save me. Instead, I grew up evil. I woke up Ko. And now he's coming here to find the river! Right here, where my mother died!"

Taking the Medallion from Relna's outstretched hand, Sparr began to sob. "Zara . . . Mother . . ."

Eric had always felt a strange ache when Zara's name was spoken. But it was nothing compared to what he felt now.

As he watched Sparr, sobbing his mother's name over and over, the king and queen and Keeah holding him up, Eric saw something they did not see.

Something no one else saw.

It nearly made his heart stop.

As Sparr clutched the Moon Medallion, the little fins that grew behind his ears shrank and dwindled away.

His fins were gone.

But when the cries of wingsnakes echoed into the passage, Sparr's grip on the Medallion loosened. It slipped from his fingers, and Relna caught it. In an instant, Sparr's fins were back, and they were burning red.

"Our time is nearly up!" said Zello.

They hurried down more stairs, turned a corner, and finally stopped in front of the room Thog had shown them before.

"The Wizard's Sneeze?" said Max.

"Why here, your majesty?" asked Khan.

"The Medallion contains Zara's spell to destroy the fountain," said Relna. "But Galen thought that one day the fountain might be needed. Before he fell completely under his own spell, he conjured something to help if Zorfendorf were ever attacked."

Neal peered into the dark room. "Did he catch a cold in here or something?"

The queen did not answer. Instead, she read from the Ring of Midnight — and the room burst with sudden light.

The stones from three of the walls floated out, lifted in the air, turned around, and slapped down on one another — *foom-foom!*

The children staggered back, amazed.

It reminded Eric of the way the fountain's stones had moved into a new shape. "They're building something!" he cried.

When the stones finally stopped moving, a giant stone head stood on wheels before them.

It was the head of Galen himself.

It bore a big stone beard, bushy eyebrows, and long curly hair. From inside the head came the sound of powerful winds rushing around, as if trying to find a way out.

And the long nose was twitching.

Max laughed. "The Wizard's Sneeze? Could it blow down Ko's palace?"

The cries of the wingsnakes became louder.

At once, the fourth wall slid away, revealing a long ramp leading up to the light.

"Care for a ride?" rumbled the head,

slowly rolling itself up the ramp. "All aboard!"

"Come on, everyone!" cried Sparr. He leaped onto the back of the platform supporting Galen's head. "Ko is attacking! My mother made the fountain for me, we can't let Ko use it! Defend it — forever!"

Eight

Big Head, Big Nose

As the children, Sparr, Max, Khan, and the king and queen rode the rolling head out from the castle, they saw Ko's black palace swooping very near the walls.

"Oh, man, here it comes!" said Julie.

It was so close they could see the angry faces of beasts peering out of the portholes.

Keeah took command. "Galen, go left!"

"Yes, yes," muttered the big head. It

turned left. Then it stopped. Its nose kept twitching.

Ko's flying palace dipped toward the walls.

"Wait . . . a bit longer . . ." said Zello.

"Not too long!" said Sparr, trembling more with every inch that the ship drew nearer.

"And now!" chirped Max. "Galen, sneeze!"

The big stone face wrinkled, the nose wiggled, the eyes shut, and the cheeks heaved.

Suddenly — *ahhh-choooo!* — an explosion of wind blew out of the face and over the walls.

Whoooom! It struck Ko's palace hard, flipping it over and over until it dipped, dropped, and finally smashed into the ground.

"Yes!" cried Eric. "Direct hit!"

The palace flipped twice again and landed upright, its walls dented, its towers crumbled.

"Unbelievable!" whispered Khan.

"You're welcome!" rumbled the stone head.

A minute went by. Two minutes. Nothing happened.

"Is it too soon to cheer?" asked Neal.

Suddenly, a large door burst open, and an army of big-boned, gray-skinned, red-eyed beasts poured out. Bringing up the rear was Ko himself, his four arms raised in rage. "ATTACKKK!" he boomed.

"Too soon!" yelled Keeah.

"Here they come!" yelled Thog from the top of the wall. "Straight to the gate —"

An instant later — *wump! wump!* — the castle's walls thundered and quaked.

The beasts were hurling themselves over and over at the gate.

"I feel another sneeze coming along," said the head. "Aim me at the gates."

Eric laughed as they wheeled the big head into position. "Sorry about this, beasts —"

Wump! The great wooden doors creaked and heaved and finally burst open.

The entrance filled with growling beasts.

"Sneeze!" yelled Keeah.

Ahhh-chooooo! A blast of air shot through the line of beasts, blowing them back in a heap of fur and scales and tails.

"Brought down by a sneeze!" cheered Neal.

"It takes a great wizard to battle beasts with just an itchy nose!" cried Khan.

"Guards!" boomed King Zello. "Attack now! Send the Red-Eyes back to their palace!"

As one, the guards gave a cheer, raised

their curved staffs, and swirled them in the air.

They charged to the gate with Zello in the lead.

Relna turned to her daughter. "Keeah, I don't want to take the risk that Ko might get the Medallion. Protect it and protect the tower. With any luck, we'll send Ko and his army straight back to the Dark Lands!"

Keeah took the Medallion, and her mother ran to the gate. "Yes! Send the beasts packing!" the princess shouted.

Max and Khan whooped as another mighty sneeze from Galen's head sent the beasts tumbling far outside the gate.

Eric cheered. "This is so awesome! Sparr, we're protecting your mother's fountain. We're keeping Ko from getting in —"

But Sparr wasn't looking at the battle.

He was squinting into the distance, his

head tilted as if he were trying to hear something.

"Sparr?" said Julie. "The gate is ours —"

"Ko isn't at the gate," said the boy. "Gethwing isn't, either. They're already inside. Everybody follow me — now!"

As the battle pushed farther outside the walls, Sparr turned and ran into the maze of streets that surrounded the castle's towers.

Eric looked at Keeah. "He knows something. I think we'd better —"

"Follow him! Right now!" said the princess. "Go!"

Eric and Keeah raced after Sparr. The others followed hard on their heels. They chased the boy through one street after another until they found Sparr standing by a deserted section of wall, staring at its big white stones.

"Oh, how could I have been so blind!" he groaned. "Ko *taught* me this trick. Look!"

He waved his hand and the wall blurred, then came clear again. This time, they saw several large stones broken on the ground and a hole in the wall five feet high.

"He's inside," said Sparr. "With Gethwing."

Suddenly, Eric caught sight of a swift movement to their left. He turned and saw the tip of a black wing edge out from around a corner.

"Ahhh!" Khan shrieked. "Him!"

It was Gethwing.

Arching up, the dark beast stretched to his full height — eight feet tall. His red eyes glowed with anger.

He made a low hissing sound. "Sparrrr!"

At that, Emperor Ko entered the alley.

"Holy cow," Julie gasped. "Runnnn!"

The kids hurried down one narrow alley after another. They zigzagged through every street around the Great Tower.

But whenever they raced down one way, Gethwing appeared at the end of it. When they turned, Ko was coming right behind them.

On and on they ran, dashing around corners into dark, shadowy lanes. At last, they entered a twisting alley from which there was no escape. With a noisy flap of his wings, Gethwing dropped in front of them. Then Ko stepped in from behind and cornered them.

"Oh, no," said Eric. His fingers sparked as he kept Gethwing at bay.

Keeah levelled both hands at Ko. Max, Khan, Neal, and Julie huddled around Sparr, protecting him.

But even as the young sorcerer tried to turn away from Ko, it was clear he couldn't. The emperor's three eyes fixed Sparr in his dark gaze. It was as if Sparr were hypnotized by the beast-master's stare.

For minutes, Ko said nothing. He moved no closer.

"What's happening?" whispered Keeah. "Why doesn't Ko try something?"

"No, it's okay if he doesn't," Neal squeaked.

Gethwing made no move, either.

Eric heard the moon dragon breathing. It was a slow, calm breath.

Gethwing's loyal to the emperor, thought Eric. *Sure. But there's something else, too. Something in his eyes. Something weird going on. What is this? Some new kind of riddle?*

Eric felt confused. He couldn't move. He knew they had to do something — but what?

Finally, Ko turned on his heels and left the children untouched and alone in the alley.

Glancing one last time at each of the

children, Gethwing leaped to the top of a building, and then he, too, was gone.

The children stood shaking in the street.

"Why did they just leave?" asked Khan.

Sparr breathed out. "Ko got what he came here for."

"But he didn't hurt us," said Keeah. "And the beasts are being pushed back. The fountain is safe. He can't get into the castle —"

"He's not going through the castle," said Sparr. "He's going through the sewers under the castle. There's a secret passage to the fountain."

Max jumped. "Who told him about that? Who even *knew* about that? Who told Ko —"

Sparr hung his head. "I did."

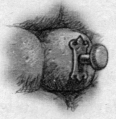

Nine

Some Things Never Change . . .

The sound of Zello's whoops, the fading clatter of sticks, and the blasts of the Wizard's Sneeze told them that the beasts were being pushed farther and farther outside the walls.

But the children stared at Sparr.

Eric couldn't believe it. "*You* told Ko about a secret passage? How could you do that?"

"How *did* you do that?" asked Keeah. "How did you even *know* about a passage?"

Sparr breathed deeply. "When you were all in the Upper World, I went back to the fountain. I tried to read that last symbol. While I was there, I discovered another of Galen's protection spells. It hid the passage that he must have used to leave the chamber once he set his own spell."

Eric stared at the boy. "Okay. But how did Ko find out about it? You didn't say a word."

Sparr looked at him. "He . . . read my thoughts. It's like he went into my head —"

"Well, get him out of there!" said Neal.

"I can't!" said Sparr, touching his fins. "Our minds are linked in a way I can't control. I wasn't like this when Ko kidnapped me. But he changed me. I'm part beast, like him. You can see that."

They heard the sound of crashing be-low them.

"The secret passage," said Julie. "Ko will find the fountain!"

Sparr's eyes glowed suddenly. "Maybe not. Ko wants the fountain and the Fifth River, but he also wants me. If I use myself as bait, and you aren't around to shield me, maybe I can lead him away. You can pro-tect the fountain! I'll go to him —"

He began to back away down the alley.

Eric's heart was racing. "No, no, no . . . this . . . this isn't right . . . no! Why does Ko want you? Gethwing said it wasn't time yet. Time for what? What will happen?"

More sounds came from below the street.

Sparr turned back. "I don't know. It hasn't happened yet. I don't know everything."

Eric remembered what had happened

to Sparr when he held the Moon Medallion. And he smiled. "Maybe that's a good thing. Look, Sparr, you're part beast. But you're not *all* beast. And you're not going back to Ko."

"But the fountain —" the boy began.

"We'll protect it together," said Julie, moving next to him. "We can do it."

"Together," said Keeah. "It's the only way we can save Droon."

Neal, Max, and Khan nodded in agreement. Everyone surrounded Sparr.

The boy looked at them all, one by one. For a long moment, he said nothing. Then he began to smile, too. "I didn't tell you that there's a good thing about Ko being in my head. . . ."

Max blinked. "There's a *good* thing?"

"Yeah," said Sparr. "Since our minds are linked, if he's in my head, I can also be in his."

Neal made a face. "I'd wear boots in there, you know. And gloves. Maybe a helmet, too."

"Oh, I'd be very careful," added Khan.

"I *am* being careful," said Sparr, closing his eyes. "And I'm delaying him. I'm throwing him off the track, for a few minutes at least. We can still get to the fountain before him. The only thing is . . . Keeah, I need the Medallion. I need it to shut down the fountain."

Keeah looked at Eric. They shared the same thought. Should Sparr have something so powerful? Could he be trusted with it?

But they already knew the answer.

"Take it," said the princess. She gave Sparr the stone, and he draped it around his neck.

"Come on, then," he said. "Into the sewers. To my mother's fountain, as fast as we can!"

And now, as they watched Sparr race down the street, everyone saw the fins behind his ears go pale and begin to get smaller.

"Whoa!" said Neal. "This is new!"

"It's the Medallion," said Eric. "It's Zara."

Keeah nodded. "I'm sure Ko's dark magic is working against him, but we have to trust that the good Sparr will win."

"The good will win," murmured Max. "We must hope it's possible!"

Sparr had already found a hole in the pavement that led to the sewers below. "Uh, excuse me up there!" he said, poking his head up from under the street. "Time is running out, you know. When Ko wants something, he gets it. Well, until — *us!*"

"Us," said Eric. "We have the power to save Droon."

"Let's make it happen," said Julie.

The six friends followed Sparr, dropping down through the street and into the sewers. They sloshed quickly through the watery tunnels that weaved under the castle.

After a few minutes, they found themselves in a tiny passage. They could go no farther. Sparr stooped in front of a small round stone with an iron knob in its center. "Yes. This is it. The entrance."

"We're in time," said Khan, sniffing in every direction. "But Ko and Gethwing are nearby and coming closer. I smell them —"

"Everybody can smell them," said Neal. "They're close, and they're mad."

Sparr pulled on the iron knob, and the little door squeaked open. "Beasts, mad? Some things never change! Come on."

Keeah squeezed through the stone doorway after Sparr. Eric followed Neal. Julie, Khan, and Max followed him.

When they reached the fountain, it was as dry as when they first saw it. The Fifth River was not flowing. The stone boat sat idle at the fountain's top. The ceiling was closed.

"There's still time," whispered Keeah.

"Use the Medallion, Sparr," said Max firmly. "And shut down the fountain."

Holding the magical stone before him, Sparr began to intone a series of strange words.

Eric turned to Sparr. "Wait, that isn't —"

Whoosh! Even though they knew the walls were still there, the children could suddenly see meadows all around them.

"Oh, my gosh," said Julie. "What is this?"

Sparr held the Medallion tightly. "Look!"

When everyone turned, they saw her.

Or a ghost of her.

Zara, Queen of Light, Sparr's mother.

"This is how it happened!" said Sparr. "I have to see it. I have to know —"

Zara's face was radiant with beauty, but her skin was pale. She seemed breathless and tired as she stumbled like a phantom over the meadows toward the kids. Her silver robes were torn, but visible on her crown was a symbol of two moons, a sun, and a snake.

Eric gasped under his breath.

Zara was clutching a small boy in her arms.

"Ahhhh!" Sparr moaned. "It's me!"

The sound of Ko and Gethwing sloshing through the sewers was closer now. But no one could look away from Zara and her son.

The queen did not see the children. She lay the young Sparr down on the ground near them, then pulled from her robe the very Moon Medallion that the older Sparr held.

"*This is for you, my son*," she whispered.

"For me!" said the older boy, watching her every move. "Oh, Mother, Mother!"

A blinding silver light flashed from the queen's Medallion, and suddenly the fountain appeared before them.

"This is how it happened!" gasped Max. "This is as it was five hundred years ago!"

Speaking softly, Zara pointed north, south, east, and west. And from each direction, a frothing, rushing river leaped over the meadows. At the last moment, the rivers dived underneath the fountain and roared up through it.

The torrent rushed straight into the sky.

"She did this to save me!" Sparr whispered.

Zara looked all around her. Then, taking her son's tiny hand, she spoke. *"Sparr, the emperor is coming. I am sending this Medallion up to your brother Urik. He will be waiting for you."*

As soon as Eric heard this, he turned to Keeah. They shared a look.

They both knew that Sparr had never left. He never made it to the safety of the Upper World.

Zara tossed the Medallion into the river.

It vanished upward through the rushing water, its silvery glow gliding through the waves and out of sight.

"Now me!" said the older Sparr, his eyes fixed on Zara. "Save me from him! Mother!"

Reaching for the younger boy, Zara faltered. She clutched her heart and sank to her knees. She fell next to the fountain.

"Sparr . . . my boy . . . my boy!"

The older Sparr fell to the floor near the ghostly image of his mother and began to weep.

Eric found that his own face was wet. Everyone stared at Sparr in amazement and sorrow.

Then, even before the vision faded, the walls seemed to reappear around them, and the chamber blazed with a sudden red light.

Black sparks sprayed across the stone floor.

And Emperor Ko burst into the chamber.

Ten

. . . And Some Things Do

Ko's horns spurted black fire, and his eyes burned with a deep red light. The air around him crackled with dark magic.

Eric stood in front of the fountain. Neal, Julie, and Max were on one side of him, Keeah and Khan on the other.

Sparr, still sobbing, trembled on his knees behind them.

The fighting seemed far away now, a

distant echo of sneezes, shrieking beasts, and clattering sticks.

When the emperor saw the motionless, nearly transparent figure of Zara on the ground, he stepped toward her.

But Sparr staggered to his feet, and the vision faded completely into the Medallion.

Ko turned. "Sparr," he said, his voice resounding in the chamber, "your mother —"

"Don't even speak her name!" Sparr yelled at the top of his lungs. "Don't say — *anything*! You will *never* get me! My mother wanted to save me from you. And she will!"

Thrusting his arm out, Sparr threw a ball of black fire at the emperor. The explosion knocked Ko to his knees. Turning, Sparr flew twenty feet across the room like a lightning bolt.

In a flash of light, he was in the stone boat.

"Sparr, wait!" Keeah cried. "Wait —"

"*Nooo!*" thundered Ko, reaching for him.

But at the top of his lungs Sparr cried out. "*YTHRA!*"

It happened in an instant. The ceiling stones swirled away, and the Fifth River burst through the fountain and blasted straight up.

Crying, sobbing, Sparr clung to the boat, water crashing around him. "Eric — here! I know you can read this! Shut down the fountain!"

He tossed the Moon Medallion to Eric as the boat crashed up the wild river and inside the tower to the sky.

"Mother, I'm coming home!" Sparr cried.

Eric grabbed the stone. He gazed after Sparr, trying to see if his fins had come back. "Wait — wait!"

Ko rushed at the fountain. "Sparr!"

"Eric, help!" Keeah pulled him around,

and together they sent a massive blast at the king of the beasts. *Blamm!* It threw Ko to the ground.

Instantly, Max spun a sticky web of silk, and Khan, Julie, and Neal heaved it over Ko.

But while the emperor was down, the dark shape of Gethwing flew into the chamber.

The dragon looked up. "The time has nearly come! I must follow —"

He leaped into the river, the water pulled him under, and he vanished out of sight.

"Stop him! Stop the river!" yelled Max.

"Close the fountain!" cried Khan.

Not knowing how he knew, not pausing to wonder, Eric read the Medallion's words and spoke the spell to shut down the fountain.

"*Prekla-temptoo-nah-sah-kee-fenn!*"

At once, a great explosion of light burst

from the fountain, throwing them all down. Ko was hurled to the far side of the room.

Thoom-thoom-thoom! The fountain's great white stones crashed down on themselves in an instant. The Fifth River trickled back into the fountain. The thundering water ceased, and the ceiling spiraled back into place.

A mound of shapeless white rock formed over the river and stopped it once and for all.

Ko staggered to his feet. He raised his four powerful arms. The fire bursting from his horns was black and wild.

He stared right at Eric, eyeing the Moon Medallion in his hands, then at the place where Zara had stood.

Everyone trembled as the beast ruler spoke.

"Zara wins this battle. Sparr escaped

me. But you shall not escape. *Selat-panoth-ra-ka-Saba!*"

Eric and Keeah raised their sparking fingertips, bracing for battle. But the gray beast turned slowly and pushed his way through the secret passage to the sewers.

Khan jumped. "A new Zorfendorf riddle! Ko says we won't escape, then he runs away!"

They heard the emperor's steps, sloshing one after another along the watery tunnels until they could hear no more.

Ko was gone.

For minutes, no one said a word.

Finally, Keeah turned to Eric. "We thought only Sparr could read the Medallion. But you know the language. . . ."

Eric felt as if his heart would explode. He stared at the silver stone in his palm, watching the words move across its surface.

"Please don't ask me how I know —"

Suddenly, Queen Relna ran into the chamber, with Zello hard on her heels.

"We did it!" she said. "The beasts are going. Ko is going. We won today —"

Neal raised his hand. "Uh, excuse me, guys, but Sparr and Gethwing —"

"You're right," said Keeah, rushing past her parents. "Mother, Father, follow us. Eric —"

"I know, I know," he said, racing after Keeah. "Sparr's in our town. With a dragon. At our beach!"

"And that girl Meredith will see all of it!" said Julie.

They all ran from the chamber into the outer passages. They raced up through the castle to the streets outside.

In the distance, Ko's black palace was wobbling away in the sky, tilting this way and that as it headed for the Dark Lands.

"That gum is still holding well," said Neal.

"Not to mention the string!" chirped Khan.

Thog came running to them. "The rainbow stairs have appeared. This way. Hurry!"

In the courtyard beside the giant tower stood the magical stairs, beaming in the afternoon light, surrounded by the townspeople and the cheering guards.

Seeing the staircase, Eric felt his heart leap. "Keeah, come with us. Max and Khan, too. We need everyone to help!"

"Then us, too!" shouted Zello, grabbing Queen Relna by the hand. "Dragons in the Upper World? Ha! I don't think so!"

They all ran for the stairs. They charged up, two steps at a time.

Eric's heart thundered in his chest. Everyone was with him now. "This is awesome! We'll get there before — before — whoa!"

The stairs shivered suddenly under his feet. He slipped, fell to his knees, and tumbled back into Neal and Keeah. They slid back, too.

All at once, the staircase began to wobble in the sky.

The steps flickered and sputtered.

Khan tripped into Max. "What's going on?"

"We'll fall off!" cried Julie, slipping on a flickering step. "Get down — down —"

A moment later, the friends tumbled back to earth and landed in a heap.

Staring up, Eric watched as, one by one, the rainbow steps began to fade. The color drained from each step until the stairs grew faint, went hazy, quivered, and finally — *plink-plink-plink!* — vanished.

Silent, stunned, everyone stared at the space where the staircase had been.

Julie breathed deeply. "But we can't stay here. Not with a moon dragon in our town!"

Max gasped. "Ko put a spell on it! He said we wouldn't escape. This is what he meant. He cursed the stairs!"

"What are we going to do?" cried Keeah.

Eric gulped. Everyone looked at him. He turned to Keeah, Max, and Khan. Then to Neal and Julie. Finally, to Queen Relna and King Zello. Then he looked at the space where the magical staircase used to be.

He thought of Sparr and Gethwing in his world.

He didn't know what to say.

Except one thing.

"Oh, no!"